SPOILERALERT!

QUESTION 1

Have **YOU** ever had a major case of **food poisoning** while **HANGING** from the edge of a **ten-metre-high** diving tower in front of your entire class, wearing nothing but rapidly **DISAPPEARING** crocheted trunks?

As seen here →

Well, I have!

QUESTION 2

Has an embarrassing **CODE-BROWN** video of YOU ever gone **VIRAL** online and now you're a world-famous **meme**, not to mention you accidentally **BLEW UP** your entire school, too?

As seen here

QUESTION 3

Have **YOU** ever been **MAROONED** on a:

a) deserted
b) haunted
c) erupting
d) all of the above

island with your arch-nemesis **AND** been chased by a **ROBOT SHARK?**

As seen here →

'D' and YES!

QUESTION 4

Have **YOU** ever been **mistaken** for a similarly named international recording superstar and teen heartthrob, and subsequently **KIDNAPPED,** requiring you to ESCAPE from a high security mansion?

As seen here →

Unfortunately, YES!

Nothing alike!

T.H.E.* JUSTIN CHASE

*Teen Heartthrob Extraordinaire

QUESTION 5

Have YOU ever been **swallowed** by a giant **SINKHOLE** and then come face to face with an INSATIABLE, ever-expanding, seemingly sentient, gargantuan **FATBERG?**

As seen here →

Feels like just yesterday!

If you answered 'YES' to all questions, congratulations. Or rather, COMMISERATIONS! You have officially had the **Worst Week Ever!**

But wait. There's **MORE?!**

BONUS QUESTION   (for extra points)

And have **YOU** ever had
to survive a **zombie**
apocalypse ...

when you live right next
door to the CEMETERY ...

FOR ELITE ATHLETES?

RUN
FOR YOUR
LIVES...

AND
BRAINS!

It's going to be one
stressful, sweaty, scary,
sporty, **SHOCKING**,
SUPERNATURAL ...

For all the brilliant booksellers and bookstores

First published in Great Britain in 2025 by Simon & Schuster UK Ltd

First published in Australia in 2024 by Scholastic Australia
An imprint of Scholastic Australia Pty Limited
PO Box 579 Gosford NSW 2250

1 3 5 7 9 10 8 6 4 2

Simon & Schuster UK Ltd
1st Floor, 222 Gray's Inn Road
London
WC1X 8HB

www.simonandschuster.co.uk
www.simonandschuster.com.au
www.simonandschuster.co.in

Simon & Schuster India, New Delhi

A CIP catalogue record for this book is available from the British Library.

PB ISBN 978-1-3985-2203-9
eBook ISBN 978-1-3985-2204-6

Typeset in Adorkable, Harimau, Kiddish, Sugary Pancake and Zakka.

Printed and Bound in the UK using 100%
Renewable Electricity at CPI Group (UK) Ltd

EVA AMORES & MATT COSGROVE

SATURDAY

Simon & Schuster

OK. LET'S START HERE!

8:03am

'WAKE UP!'

So far this woeful week I've been woken up by ...

1. MY MUM ON MONDAY

with her dreaded, patented
LIGHT SWITCH FLICK.

ANNOYMENT FACTOR:
Four and a half light bulbs

WAKE UP!

CLICK

2. MY DAD ON TUESDAY

with a side-serving of slobber,

courtesy of NICKERS.

DOG DROOL FACTOR:
Bring an umbrella

3. MY ARCH-ENEMY

(Slash Current Step-Brother!)

MARVIN ON WEDNESDAY

FEAR FACTOR:
Four fins

4. TV HOSTS ON THURSDAY

live and televised in high-definition.

MORTIFICATION FACTOR:
International

5. MYSELF ON FRIDAY

except I wasn't even asleep!

PAIN FACTOR:
A pinch and two slaps

But today, **SATURDAY,** I'm woken by a gentle voice coaxing me out from a foggy slumber.

'WAKE UP, Justin!'

My eyelids flicker open. A kind face, filled with compassion, is floating above me. It's my friend, Mia. Eyes wide with concern. Looking softly down on me.

Like an angel

Me, with sleep **CRUD** clogging my eyes.

What even is this stuff?!

Me, with my **bed hair** resembling a shambolic bird's nest.

TWEET TWEET*

*My new home!

Me, with a rivulet of congealed **SALIVA** trickling from the side of my mouth.

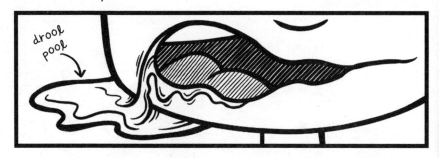

drool pool

Me, clutching my **Cloppy Doppy** plush toy to my cheek like a baby with a blankie.

I'm suddenly very **awake** and very **AWARE** of how I must look to Mia right now. That's **NOT** the impression I want to be making!

My mind is racing through my options in this moment ...

OPTION A:

Shut my eyes and pretend I'm still asleep.

Nan calls this 'PLAYING POSSUM'.

ZZZZZZZZZ

OPTION B:

Smile dreamily and say something witty/charming/funny –
except I can't think of ANYTHING witty/charming/funny to
say! Dad's kind of funny. What would he say?

Sit bolt upright, emit a high-pitched **SHRIEK** and then jump out of bed, flinging **Cloppy Doppy** across the room like a lumpy frisbee while simultaneously trying to pat my hair down, wipe my mouth and rub my eyes.

EEEEKKKKK!

PAT

FLING

RUB

WIPE

My brain unfortunately chooses **OPTION C!** Why?

'Oi! Keep it down, Poo Boy. I'm creating **magic** here.'

That's Marvin, over on his half (more like three quarters!) of our room. I can't believe that BOTHERSOME, two-faced bully is now officially my **step brother!** Of all the people – and even inanimate objects – on the planet, he would have been my **LAST** choice for a brother!

PREFERABLE OPTIONS FOR A BROTHER:

T.H.E.
Justin Chase

Less money spent on name labels!

A life-size cardboard cutout of Marvin

Less annoying.
Better personality.

A random cactus

Less prickly.
Better personality.

Marvin glares at me **ICILY**, **HUFFS** in contempt and then turns back to his computer and continues **tapping** away at his keyboard, extra loudly.

I ignore him and turn to Mia. I'm **embarrassed**, but also very **CONFUSED**.

'What happened last night?' I ask her groggily. 'The last thing I remember was being in the **cemetery**.

It was **CREEPY!** ← ALL CAPS CREEPY!

There were cats **EVERYWHERE**, just **NOT** Captain Fluffykins.

And then I **stumbled**. I **FELL!** There were **GOOSEBUMPS!**

I CALLED OUT FOR A HAND AND THEN . . .'

'Yes, yes. We were there,' Marvin **butts** in. 'We heard you scream like the nappy-wearing **INFANT** you are and then we found you. I've already uploaded the video on my channel. It's getting good numbers. Let's watch.'

Marvin hits **PLAY** on ...

SOME SELECTED HIGHLIGHTS

← Actually LOWLIGHTS is more accurate

OPENING SHOT:

There I am, **unconscious** on the ground. Mia is kneeling by my side gently shaking me.

Oh, I am out **COLD!**
Please note Marvin is doing
absolutely **NOTHING!**

Extreme
booger
closeup!

I take that back.
Marvin is **zooming** in
UP my nostrils!

And now he's prodding
my head with his **FOOT!**
REPEATEDLY!

KNOCK
KNOCK
KNOCK

And now he's re-enacting
the Justin Chase video clip
for 'Let Me In'!

It gets **WORSE!**
Now he's fixing his hair and
looking straight to camera.
It's about to be a ...

19

MARVELOUS MARVIN
MONOLOGUE

TRANSCRIPT:

Hello, devoted fans. Yes, I'm here in a derelict cemetery at midnight, bravely risking my life, searching for Poo Boy's mangy, feral cat.

And how does Poo Boy repay my selflessness? He's taking a nap. Fast asleep. Is it past someone's beddy-byes time? Pathetic!

Thankfully Mia interjects

We need to get Justin home!

Fine. I am feeling the chill. Let's go. You drag him. I'll continue documenting this moment for my fans.

THAT'S NOT FAIR

I agree. It's not fair. Once again I'm doing the real heavy-lifting. Providing lighting, atmosphere and sparkling commentary while you just lug the dead weight.

YOU ARE amazing, YOU GREAT BIG SACK OF raw talent.

YOU BETTER sign an autograph for me RIGHT NOW. I SWEAR I WILL like and subscribe. I REALLY CARE ABOUT YOUR brilliant CHANNEL. NOW GRAB HIS LEGS.

I bet Marvin has edited Mia's voice in the video! That sneak. He probably used A.I. Don't believe everything you see – or hear – on the internet!

Well, I suppose I already carry him with my talent, I may as well literally carry him. I am truly noble.

Oh, no. I think my pants are...

It feels like I'm watching in S L O W   M O T I O N as Marvin grabs my leg to 'help' lift me and inadvertently (or absolutely intentionally!) **PULLS MY PANTS DOWN.**

Wait! It *is* in S L O W   M O T I O N on the video Marvin has edited. And now he's freeze framed and **ZOOMED IN**. And there they are. My undies on display to the whole wide world **AGAIN!**

Worst step-brother EVER!

Ha! If you think Poo Boy is too old to be wearing Cloppy Doppy undies let me know in the comments!

At this stage I may as well just take out a **billboard** for ...

*Back-up Lucky Undies** (actual Lucky Undies are in the wash)
**Evidently not THAT lucky!

I'm as red as a **TOMATO**, equal parts **anger** and **embarrassment**. I'm absolutely **FUMING** at Marvin.

He's smiling **smugly** in return. 'In case you're interested Poo Boy, in my **online poll 89%** of people DO think you're too old to be wearing Cloppy Doppy underwear.'

I push past Marvin to take control of his computer so I can **FAST FORWARD** to the end, but there's nothing to see except me being carried/dragged back home like a **sack of potatoes**, repeatedly getting my head **BUMPED** on ...

HEADSTONES

GATES

DOORWAYS

STAIRS

No wonder my head **HURTS!**

MY BRAIN BEFORE

MY BRAIN AFTER

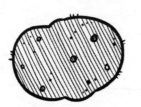

Mashed potato!

'OK. So you brought me back here. I get that, and I've got the bumps to prove it, but what about ... (and I can't quite believe I'm about to say this) ... **THE ZOMBIE?!**'

'**THE ZOMBIE?!?!**' the others echo.

Marvin is looking at me like I'm from another planet.

SHOCK and BEWILDERMENT

UFJ (Unidentified Flying Justin)

Mia is looking at me like Dad looks at a broken **toilet**.

CONCERN and TENDERNESS

Poor thing!

25

'What do you mean **"the zombie"**?' they ask in unison.

'You know! **ZOMBIE!!**' How can I make it any clearer?

'Walk like **THIS.**'

'Eat **BRAINS** ...'

I'LL have the frontal lobe with a side of cerebral cortex.

BRAINS 'R' US
MENU

'A reanimated human body given life by a supernatural force'

Official definition! (Usually on the last page!)

DICTIONARY

'You saw a **zombie** in the cemetery?' Mia asks, baffled.

'Well, I saw a **HAND!**' I offer weakly.

Marvin is rolling his eyes so much I think they've done a complete 360 degree rotation!

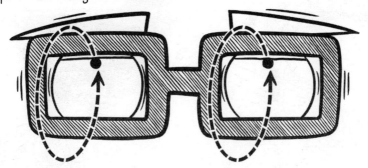

I'm starting to doubt my own **SANITY**. (Which is really saying something as the owner of a cat most likely abducted by aliens.) But I **DID** see a hand. I try to convince the others by re-enacting the scene.

'There was a hand that burst out of the ground. Like this!'

Not buying it!

My limited theatrical abilities don't seem up to the task. (FYI: I was cast as Tree Number 3 in my last school play, and even then, the drama teacher **cut** my only line!)

I'm waving my hand desperately, flailing about the room like a sockless sock-puppeteer. The Safety Science Sock Puppets would be **AGHAST!**

I can tell Mia and Marvin don't believe me and my hand or Ducky, Mr Wolf or even **BUNNY WUNNY!**

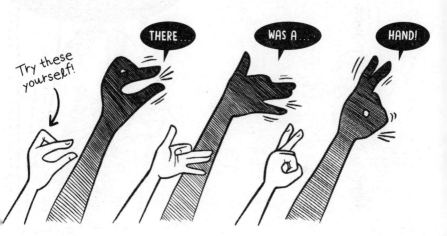

'I'm not making it up! I'm CERTAIN I saw a **ZOMBIE HAND** last night at the cemetery!' I gesture out the window that looks onto the **Cemetery For Elite Athletes** at the back of our house.

Marvin is rolling his eyes **AGAIN** while Mia is calmly trying to **reassure** me as we go over to the window.

Together they say: 'There's no such thing as ...'

'ZOMBIES!'

The backyard is overrun with ambling ZOMBIES. I feel strangely **validated** but also incredibly ...

TERRIFIED!

Dialing up the TERROR, our collective **SCREAM** seems to have caught the attention of the zombies. In **unison**, they turn their heads in our direction, their GHOULISH, glowing eyes staring blankly at us.

At least they're **down there** and we're **SAFE** up here!

INCORRECT

From out of the ghastly **HORDE** emerges
a lycra-clad zombie running straight
towards us at full speed. Carrying a giant
POLE. Which is **weird**. Well, the whole
zombie **APOCALYPSE** in my backyard is
weird, but the pole just elevates it to a
higher level of **WEIRDNESS**.

   Speaking of
higher levels ...

The **ZOMBIE** has now planted the end of the pole into the ground ....

Slow motion
lycra is never
a good idea.
Look away!

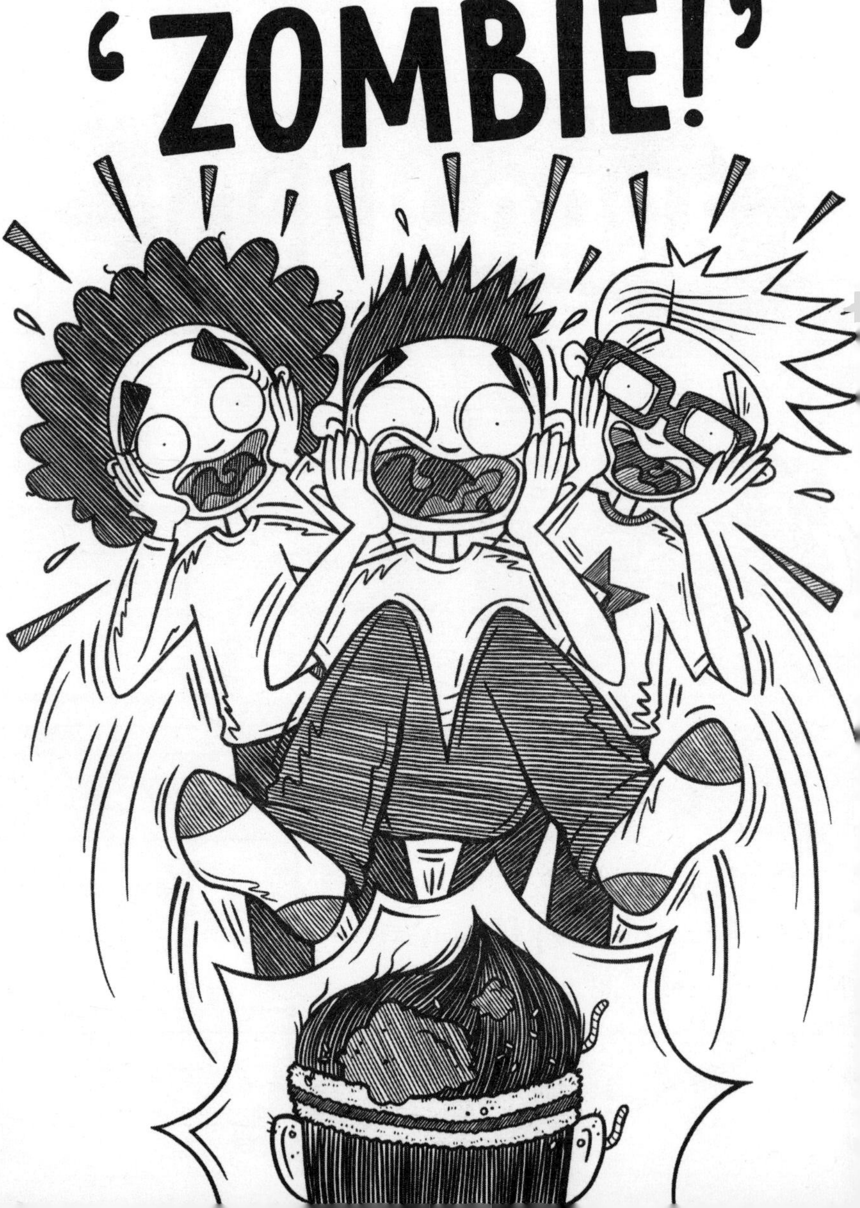
'ZOMBIE!'

The pole-vaulting **zombie** lands with the grace of an elite athlete, rolling onto the floor and then SPRINGING to their feet. I'm **almost** impressed. I'm also **almost PEEING** my pants as the zombie LUNGES towards us.

BRAAAIIINS!

'She's got BRAINS. Smartest in the class!' Marvin pushes Mia forwards as he **DARTS** down the stairs out of our room. Mia and I are right behind him.

Unfortunately, the zombie is right behind US!

We're now reluctantly playing a game of ...

ZOM NOM NOM!

Where we're the '**NOM-NOM**' part!

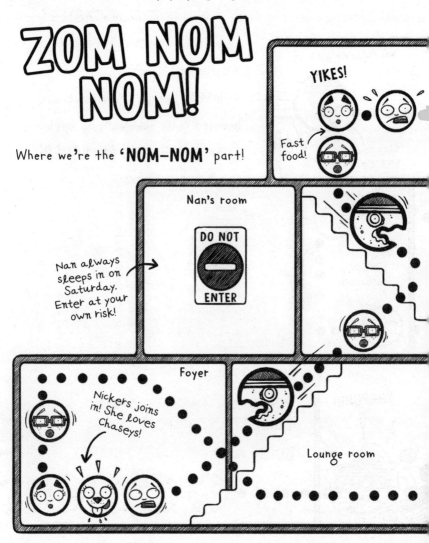

YIKES!

Fast food!

Nan's room

DO NOT — ENTER

Nan always sleeps in on Saturday. Enter at your own risk!

Foyer

Nickers joins in! She loves Chaseys!

Lounge room

My/Marvin's room

On an all-you-can-eat mission!

It's like a case of **CHASEYS** through the house, with very strong **motivation** not to become 'IT', with 'IT' being a breakfast brain **burrito** for a pole-vaulting zombie! I like my brain **UN-MUNCHED!**

Bathroom

Dad's room

DO NOT ENTER

Under strict instructions from Dad. He needs his rest after fighting fatbergs.

RAARGHH!

Kitchen

Laundry

With our zombie **pursuer** currently TANGLED in Nan's crochet wool pile, we **BURST** out the back door to SAFETY.

This is **NOT** safety! This is the **OPPOSITE** of safety. This is **unsafe** to the extreme. This is about as safe as ...

Taking candy from a stranger in an unmarked van.

Running with scissors on concrete, blindfolded in thongs.

Going to the bathroom immediately after Dad on Curry Night.

Swimming outside the flags DIRECTLY after eating, with no sunscreen!

Hand-feeding a lion (who hasn't eaten for a week) a bucket of Pecky's Chook Shack drumsticks while dressed as the Pecky's Chook Shack chicken mascot.

Stunt jumping over a gorge filled with venomous snakes through a ring of fire while wearing a highly flammable polyester cape and no helmet!

 13 TRILLION!

Unlucky number

Very big number

We are surrounded by ...

'A LOT OF ZOMBIES!'

I should probably mention I'm a bit of a zombie **EXPERT**. I've seen* a lot of zombie **MOVIES** (well at least three and three quarters – one got a bit too scary to watch all the way to the end!) so I know a thing or two about zombies.

FLASHBACK

* Snuck in watching them when Dad fell asleep on the sofa

Blanket for extra protection

But these aren't **regular** zombies!

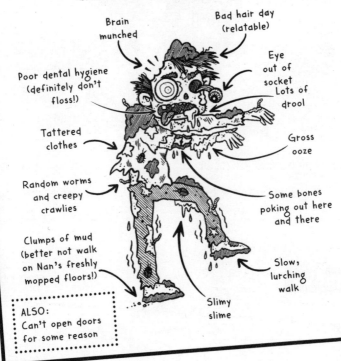

REGULAR ZOMBIES
as seen in the B-grade movies

Brain munched

Bad hair day (relatable)

Poor dental hygiene (definitely don't floss!)

Eye out of socket

Lots of drool

Tattered clothes

Gross ooze

Random worms and creepy crawlies

Some bones poking out here and there

Clumps of mud (better not walk on Nan's freshly mopped floors!)

Slow, lurching walk

ALSO:
Can't open doors for some reason

Slimy slime

THE DIFFERENCE?

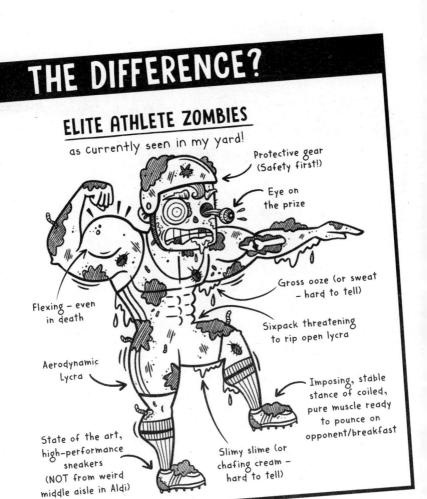

ELITE ATHLETE ZOMBIES
as currently seen in my yard!

Protective gear
(Safety first!)

Eye on
the prize

Gross ooze (or sweat
– hard to tell)

Flexing – even
in death

Sixpack threatening
to rip open lycra

Aerodynamic
Lycra

Imposing, stable
stance of coiled,
pure muscle ready
to pounce on
opponent/breakfast

State of the art,
high-performance
sneakers
(NOT from weird
middle aisle in Aldi)

Slimy slime (or
chafing cream –
hard to tell)

These are ELITE ATHLETE ZOMBIES!

Heaps of them. In all impressive shapes and weight divisions.

And they're **ARMED!** (At least the ones with arms still attached.) They're **wielding** their sporting equipment like WEAPONS! There are ...

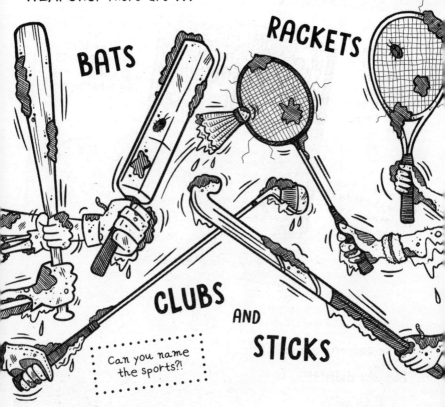

BATS

RACKETS

CLUBS

AND

STICKS

Can you name the sports?!

... all raised MENACINGLY into the air. Even a **PING PONG PADDLE** is pretty **intimidating** when a zombie's waving it in your general direction!

I am certainly **NOT** physically equipped or mentally prepared to deal with this zombie **THREAT**. Maybe if Mum had let me play **THIS**

Best-selling video game that officially catapulted the MMBBSS franchise into the stratosphere

Voted Number 1 classic greatest game of all time

The alien viking skeleton robots have to destroy an army of rabid zombies

Asked for this for my birthday, Christmas and even Easter. DENIED every time!

Rated Z (for Zapping Zombies)

... I would have sufficient training and the experience to deal with the current zombie **INFESTATION** situation.

But she **didn't**!

So I **DON'T**!

Thanks, Mum! (said sarcastically.) Once again, **ruining** my life by denying me video game access!

TOO MANY VIDEO GAMES!

Correction. Not ENOUGH video games!!

I think it might be **safer** inside with one zombie than outside with a cemetery's worth of them. We quickly **DASH** back in the house and **SLAM** the door shut.

The pole-vaulter zombie is almost **untangled** from the wool so we **BOLT** past them and back up the stairs where we run into **Dad**. He's been turned into a **ZOMBIE!**

Vacant stare

BRGHJMHHS

Drool

Incomprehensible groaning

Foul stench of decay

Unsteady gait

Hang on. He's **fine**. Just half asleep and lumbering to the bathroom. 'Keep it down, kiddos. It's the **WEEKEND**,' he yawns, before locking himself in the bathroom.

First toilet visit of the morning means we won't be seeing Dad again for **at least** twenty minutes, so he's not going to save us from the zombie!

There's no help from Marjorie/step-mum either!

Barely awake

NO RUNNING IN THE HALLWAY!

... she yells out from the bedroom in total **school-principal-on-auto-pilot** mode.

SCHOOL PRINCIPAL ON AUTO-PILOT SCRIPT:

- No running in the hallway.
- No running on the concrete.
- No running in the classroom.
- No running on the steps.
- Inside voices only!
- Attention please, students.
- Eyes to the front.
- Hands off. Feet off.
- Please stop chewing the collar of your shirt while humming and doodling in the margins of your workbook when you're supposed to be completing your maths assignment!

They really don't like running!

Always said with a distinctly OUTSIDE voice!

Umm... maybe that was just my principal to me!

What does your School Principal always say?

Write it here

Draw them here

Nan's still soundly **asleep**, just when we need her famous walking stick **WHACKING** skills to fight off our zombie ...

Sound asleep

ZZZZZzzzZZZZzzzZZZZZZZZZ

... so we **RACE** back upstairs to my/Marvin's room. There's nowhere else to go though. Our only option now is to **HIDE!**

Mia goes for the **wardrobe**. Marvin goes for his **cutouts**.

I can't fit in! (It's jammed with Marvin's merch!)

I don't fit in! (Marvin points out I don't have his star quality!)

I'm panicking with the **PRESSURE** of finding a good hiding place. I've always been terrible at **hide and seek!**

FLASHBACK

Back when Captain Fluffykins was cute

Eyes tightly shut so no-one can see me!

Kitty Litter Tray

All the decent spots are already taken. I've only got three LOUSY options ...

WORST AVAILABLE HIDING SPOTS EVER!

The lampshade   The chair   The curtain

Wait! I forgot the classic: UNDER THE BED! I dive under, bringing Cloppy Doppy with me for protection, and **commando crawl** through the **CLUTTER** to the back.

I can hear footsteps pounding up the steps. Too fast to be Dad. Too heavy to Marjorie or Nan. The zombie is **BACK!**

I'll just be completely QUIET. I hold my breath. Not a single sound. Just me shaking from fear in total **silence.**

KA-CHING! KA-CHING!

It's MUM calling on my phone. Why now? She ALWAYS has the **WORST TIMING!**

EXHIBIT A.
Interrupting a mega important mutli-player online game at the most critical moment.

EXHIBIT B.
Whipping the changing room curtains wide open to see if my pants fit before I've even pulled them up.

EXHIBIT C.
Butting in when I'm on a VC with my mates with an embarrassing and unnecessary question.

I fumble to silence the phone but accidentally hit **answer**.

Mum appears on the screen.

Where are you?

Are you under the bed?

There will be dust mites under the bed.

There's definitely dust bunnies!

Get out from there!

Yes Mum

Me whispering!

I can't talk now

I can't hear you!

I can't talk right now.

Stop mumbling!

Whispering louder

I CAN'T TALK RIGHT NOW

Speak up!!

Whisper shouting

I CAN'T TALK RIGHT NOW BECAUSE I'M ABOUT TO HAVE MY BRAINS EATEN BY A ZOMBIE!

PUT THAT ZOMBIE ON THE PHONE! WHAT IS GOING ON? WHERE IS YOUR FATHER?! I'M COMING THERE RIGHT NOW!

I shouldn't have whisper shouted! The zombie's face appears, **peering** under the bed towards my hiding spot.

Me screaming! 'AAARRGGHHH!'

51

Luckily the pole-vaulter zombie is too **BIG** and **muscular** to fit under the bed. They're **WEDGED** at the edge unable to get any further, like when Captain Fluffykins got stuck in Nicker's dog door at our old place.

FLASHBACK

REOW*

*I will remember this indignity!

The zombie's arm is trying to grab me but I'm just out of reach! I throw my **PHONE** in self defence ...

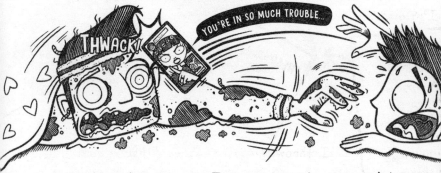

THWACK!

YOU'RE IN SO MUCH TROUBLE...

... and then whatever else I can get my hands on. A box of my old toys and other junk gives me plenty of **AMMUNITION**.

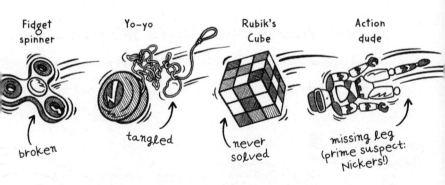

Fidget spinner — broken

Yo-yo — tangled

Rubik's Cube — never solved

Action dude — missing leg (prime suspect: Nickers!)

Don't judge me but I also throw **Cloppy Doppy**. The Zombie catches C.D. then moans **'BRAAAINNNS'** before CHEWING his head right off!

BEFORE

AFTER

RIP CLOPPY DOPPY!

I am **SCARED!** I'm also ...

- afraid
- alarmed
- anxious
- fearful
- frightened
- panicky
- petrified
- shaken
- startled
- terrified

as seen here

THESAURUS

WHOOOOOOOOOOOOSH!

I throw my trusty, dusty **BOOK**, as big as a brick, but it does **nothing**. The zombie keeps **SWIPING** their brawny arm, trying to reach me.

This whole thing is **SCARIER** than ...

The HORROR!

• The **BATHTUB** after Dad when he's had a **rough** day at the office – and his office is the **SEWER!**

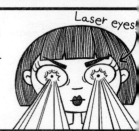
Laser eyes!

• Mum's **expression** when I remember on Sunday night that I have a school project due the next day and I haven't started and I need glue and we don't have glue.

• A robot shark.

• A holographic pirate ghost.

• **A HOLOGRAPHIC ROBOT PIRATE SHARK GHOST!**

I'm running out of **projectiles**.
All that's left is my box of treasured
swimming TROPHIES. I grab one.
Ahhh, my first 200 metres freestyle
trophy. What a special day!

FLASHBACK

I don't **really** want to throw my trophy, but I also
REALLY don't want that zombie EATING my ...

BRAAAIIINS!

I **HURL** the golden trophy. It **sparkles** and SPINS through the air, heading straight for the zombie's forehead.

But before the trophy hits its **target,** the zombie catches it. Their expressions changes and now they're moaning ...

TROOOOPHY!

The zombie appears to have totally forgotten about me and my **delicious brain** and is proudly clutching the trophy. I **SNEAK** past while they're happily distracted.

'Guys! Let's get out of here,' I whisper.

Mia peeks out from the wardrobe and Marvin appears from behind his cutouts.

I gesture towards the steps. 'Go! We're safe now!'

INCORRECT

Our getaway exit down the stairs is **BLOCKED** by ...

'MORE ZOMBIES!'

A whole **squad** of drooling zombies is chasing Nickers, who is having the time of her life, up into the room.

We're **TRAPPED** and **outnumbered** by the zombies!
I think this is **GAME OVER!**

And then Nickers spots the shiny TROPHY!

WOOF**

** TREASURE! Target locked.

She bounds across the room and **SNATCHES** it right out of the pole-vaulter zombie's hand ...

YOINK!

WOOF***

*** Oh. It's just small human's worthless treasure!

... and gives it back to **ME!**

WOOF****

**** You can have it. Got any socks?

Dog drool

Zombie drool

JUSTIN CHASE

And then **ALL** the zombies spot the shiny TROPHY!

For the first time in my life I **don't** want to be holding the trophy. The zombies, meanwhile, DEFINITELY do! They start **advancing** towards me.

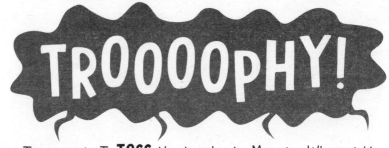

TROOOOPHY!

In a panic I **TOSS** the trophy to Marvin. Who quickly **THROWS** it to Mia. Who **CHUCKS** it back to me, like we're playing HOT POTATO!

The zombies really want the trophy so I throw the trophy straight at them ...

It's all yours!

... but **MISS!** Adding to my lifelong string of missing.

CLOSE (AND NOT SO CLOSE) ENCOUNTERS!

The bin	The toilet	The goals

The trophy goes **sailing** out the window.

WHOOOOOOOSH!

Thankfully, the zombies FOLLOW it!

We rush to the window to watch the huge zombie

STACKS ON!

They SQUABBLE over the
trophy like seagulls over a chip,

SQUWARK! SQUWARK!

or bargain-hunting shoppers
over the last discounted item,

SQUWARK! SQUWARK!

or elite athlete zombies over a
shiny gold (plated!) trophy.

I can relate! I'm a fan of any **positive reinforcement** but NOTHING beats a **TROPHY!**

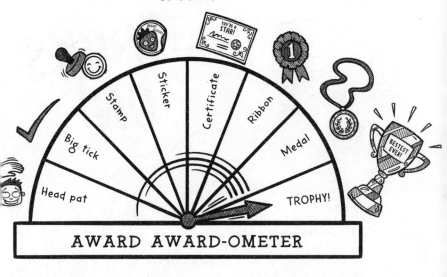

Big tick

Stamp

Sticker

Certificate

Ribbon

Medal

Head pat

TROPHY!

BESTEST EVER!

AWARD AWARD-OMETER

As we observe the **SCRAMBLE** below, Mia pipes up.

'I think their elite athlete side's natural desire for a trophy is **outweighing** their zombie side's unnatural desire for a brain snack!' she **hypothesises.** 'We might be able to use that information to our advantage.'

Just not right now because we've been **spotted** again!

A troupe of zombie **GYMNASTS** are currently LAUNCHING themselves through the air at us. There's ...

STRADDLING

TUCKING

PIKING ↑

AND WHATEVER THIS IS!

So graceful, yet utterly TERRIFYING when it's heading straight for **YOU!**

'BLOCK THE WINDOWS!'

We manage to **drag** my mattress and butt it up against the window – just in time to **BOUNCE** the gymnasts back.

We quickly **BLOCK** the other window with Marvin's mattress so now we're safely **barricaded** in our room.

Then we hear **MOANING** coming up the steps! Relax. (For now!) Not zombies. Dad, Marjorie and Nan are finally awake and have come to investigate the **RUCKUS**.

We attempt to explain but **nothing** makes sense. Instead we cautiously **PEEL** back my mattress from the window so they can see for themselves.

'ZOMBIES!'

They **JAM** the mattress back up against the window.

'I wasn't expecting that!' Dad exclaims. **'ZOMBIES** are way down on my list!'

Nan is **swearing** up a storm. The swear jar is going to be overflowing!

Marjorie tries calling all the emergency numbers and authorities but is only getting **automated messages.**

I think Nan is finally out of swear words. 'Maybe we should make a cup of tea and check the **NEWS!**' she suggests.

LIVE FROM THE NEWSDESK

In our lead story today, the entire world breathes a collective sigh of relief as international recording superstar and teen heartthrob Justin Chase is discharged from hospital fully recovered from his toilet-related injury.

Fans held a candlelight vigil outside the hunk's hospital, praying for his beautiful, chiselled face.

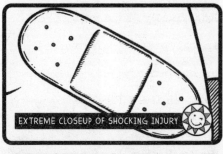

In other chiselled-face news — Mount Rushmore is now less 'Rush' and more 'Cats' as all the presidents' famous faces mysteriously morphed to felines overnight. This follows on from similar monumental cat-astrophes around the world this week.

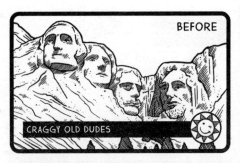

And finally, a zombie apocalypse appears to be happening right now, entirely localised to the small town of Wally Valley, the home of the internet sensation known only as Pool Boy. Coincidence? Probably.

And that's the news!

So the GOOD news is T.H.E. Justin Chase's face is fine.

The BAD news is, officially, we're dealing with a ...

ZOMBIE APOCALYPSE!

Ominous lightning

Surprisingly, Dad is stepping up in this moment, shouting orders like an angry DRILL SERGEANT from a **war movie**!

'SECURE THE PERIMETERS!'

SAFETY FIRST!

APPROVED BY S.S.S.P.*

*SAFETY SCIENCE SOCK PUPPETS

TRANSLATION: We need to zombie-proof this house while we work on a proper getaway plan!

'INVENTORY CHECK!'

A lot of shouty spittle spray

TRANSLATION: What supplies do we have at our disposal that we can use against our zombie attackers?

A quick **stocktake** of the house shows that we have an

ABUNDANCE of ...

☑ TOILET PAPER

Dad really bought in bulk!

Excess supplies from the
toilet-themed wedding

☑ LEFTOVER SMOOTHIE

Dad over-estimated demand

Snot green

NONE of the guests
went back for a top up

☑ CROCHET WOOL

For the rug we're making together

Nan buys it on sale and
hoards it in the cupboard

☑ MARVIN'S CUTOUTS

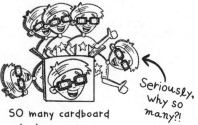

Seriously, why so many?!

SO many cardboard
cutouts.

☑ BALLOONS

FLASHBACK

MR POOPY
THE PLUMBING
CLOWN

Balloon poos not quite as cute as balloon animals

From one of Dad's
abandoned business ideas

So, we will do what we can with what we have!

Commence ... **OPERATION: ZOMBIE BLOCK!**

First Line of defence. ROLL OUT!

1. T.P. TORPEDOES

TOILET PAPER

US

ZOMBIES

We launch an unrelenting **BARRAGE** of loo rolls out the windows at the approaching zombies.

FOOOOOSH!

SUCCESS!

The zombies are **TANGLED** in the toilet paper and can't see where they are going!

We throw balloons filled with all the **diabolical** kale, cucumber and cabbage sensation cleansing smoothie. They **BURST** on impact in an **explosion** of green **GOOP!**

Even the zombies (who, may I remind you, eat **BRAINS!**) are **REPULSED** by Dad's concoction!

And as an added bonus, the house walls are now coated in **slime** and are too slippery to climb. The ground is **SLUSH**. The zombies can't get a grip and are **slipping** and **SLIDING** everywhere.

STEP 1

We use all the cardboard cutouts of Marvin to **LURE** the zombies.

Nan is crocheting at double speed to make the **nets**.

STEP 2

And then we **TRAP** the zombies in a **SNARE**. Just like in the cartoons!

There are **netted** zombies hanging all around the house, strung up like wiggling bags of oranges.

So far, so good. We're managing to hold back the zombie **SURGE**. For now! But they just keep coming (we do live next to a cemetery!) and we're running out of supplies and ideas.

4 . . . .

What would YOU do?

Design your own zombie defence or trap here.

Seriously, we need all the help we can get!

So Phase 1: **SECURE THE PERIMETERS** is complete. Time to move on to Phase 2 ...

'EVACUATE ASAP!'

TRANSLATION: We need to get outta here. FAST!

I am 100% behind Phase 2! But **where** do we go and **how** do we get there?

WHERE?

I KNOW!

DING!

The news said the zombie apocalypse was **localised** to Wally Valley. In zombie movies, people **always** go to **'HIGHER GROUND'**. I can't think of anywhere higher nearby than WALLY HEIGHTS!

If we could get to Princess' high-security **mansion**, we would have high-security (better than toilet paper torpedoes) **PLUS** a getaway HELICOPTER!

Wally Heights

76

HOW?

I DON'T know!

We won't **ALL** fit in Dad's toilet truck. Including Mia's family next door, (we can't leave them behind) there's nine of us all together. Ten if you count Nickers! And I do!!

We need a **BUS!**

EVACUEES LIST

- ME
- Dad
- Nan
- Marjorie
- Marvin
- Mia
- Mia's mum
- Mia's dad
- Mia's bro
- Nickers

DING!

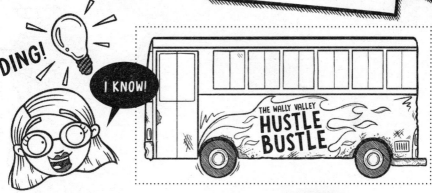

I KNOW!

THE WALLY VALLEY
HUSTLE BUSTLE

Marjorie puts in a call to the Wally Valley Hustle Bustle special emergency **HOTLINE**. A secret number only available to top customers. And with all those excursions and sporting trips, School Principal Ms King is **THE** top customer.

I'M ON MY WAY, BOSS!

Betty Bus Driver

77

A peek out the window reveals there are even **MORE** zombies surrounding us now. I'm not sure how we'll even get past them and onto the bus when it gets here.

BRAINSTORMING doesn't help with a solution.

Maybe there's been an update on the **ZS*** on the **TV** ...

* Zombie Situation

10:00am

I'm Kerry.

And I'm Perry.

Welcome to this bonus extended edition of WAKE UP as we broadcast live from Wally Valley.

Home of Pool Boy AND now the Zombie Apocalypse. Brought to you by Pecky's Chook Shack.

There's our house in the background!

Love that chicken salt!

LIVE

CAUTION

DO NOT CROSS

ZOMBIE APOCALYPSE IN PROGRESS

TRY PECKY'S CHOOK SHACK'S APOCALYPTIC SPECIAL SAUCE!

Overnight it appears the residents of The Cemetery For Elite Athletes decided to vacate their premises and are now spilling out into the neighbourhood.

As you can see, authorities have cordoned off the area behind us. Nobody in or out!

WE'LL SEE ABOUT THAT!

I recognise that voice!

79

And, indeed, no police tape or zombie **can** stop Mum.

I race to the window to watch Mum (trailed by Step-Vlad) **FIGHT** her way through the zombie athletes using her martial arts moves.

SCENE DELETED

BY THE CENSORS

(I WARNED YOU. DO NOT MESS WITH MUM!)

Please enjoy these wholesome, delicious food items instead ...

SCENE DELETED

BY THE CENSORS

(OH, MUM IS REALLY LETTING THE ZOMBIES HAVE IT!)

Now imagine the same items dropped from a great height ...

Apologies for the disruption to transmission.
We now resume our scheduled programming ...

While Mum is making **scrambled** eggs and tomato PASTE out of the zombies, Vlad **DUCKS** and WEAVES with his lightning-fast reflexes. They clear a path through the **scrum** of zombies and make it to the house.

Mum **bursts** through the front door and it is **HUG TIME!**

Emotional air-blocking embrace

Dispassionate, no-contact pat

Replacement allergy bracelet (and tracking device!)

Ignore the zombie juice

I'm so **relieved** Mum is here. It's always **SAFER** with Mum around. No offence, Dad! Just different parenting styles and approaches to personal safety ... and **gravity!**

I'm even happy to see **Vlad**. Maybe he can call on his dark army of fellow **VAMPIRES** to battle the zombies!

THAT would be a fair fight!

Unlike the current **situation** ...

POOR, DEFENCELESS REGULAR TWELVE-YEAR-OLD KID (WHO COULD PASS FOR TEN) PLUS MISCELLANEOUS FAMILY, FRIEND AND NEIGHBOURS **VS ZOMBIES**

We need to hold back the zombies somehow while we wait for the bus. Mum can't karate **CHOP** them all. There's just too many. And now they're **POUNDING** on the doors!

DING!

I KNOW!

Looks like Mia has come up with a **PLAN**. Even better, it doesn't require a **vampire army!**

'I've been observing the zombies. They are **still** elite athletes at heart. It's in their **DNA**. They **WANT** to compete. They want to **WIN**. And watching them fight Justin's Mum — they play by the **RULES**.

We were able to get past that pole-vaulter zombie with one little trophy. Imagine what we could do with ...'

11:12am

COLOUR BY NUMBER
1 = GOLD

You might need a few gold pencils for this one!

So shiny!

It took a while and a **LOT** of **superglue** and every single
one of my swimming trophies and medals . . .

So many
momentous
moments!

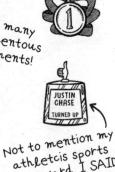

Not to mention my
athletcis sports
day award. I SAID
don't mention it!

PLUS Marvin's trophies . . .

AKA Teacher's
Pet Award!
BLEEERGH!

PLUS Nan's and Dad's trophies . . .

Dad was runner-
up to Plumby Pete
– and he's still
bitter about it!

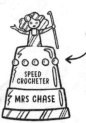

The coveted
Golden Dunny
Dolly. The
competition
couldn't even
get close to
Nan!

(But just imagine
if we had access
to Mum's trophy
cabinet!)

to create this **irresistible**, tantalising **PRIZE** for . . .

THE
ZOMBIE GAMES!

OK. Not the most creative name but we were under pressure!

WANNA WIN THIS?

YEAH, YOU DO!

THE ULTIMATE SUPER DUPER MEGA TROPHY

SO MUCH BETTER THAN BRAINS!

ARE YOU AN ELITE ATHLETE AND/OR ZOMBIE LOOKING FOR SPORTING GLORY?

  LOOK NO FURTHER!

 SIGN UP NOW FOR THE HUMANS VS ZOMBIES GAMES!

FORGET ALL ABOUT BRAINS AND FOCUS ON WINNING GOLD!

Flyers printed on Marvin's printer and dropped out the window

We've got the zombies' **attention!** They are super **KEEN** for the ZOMBIE GAMES and a crack at that trophy! The zombies are lined up in formation outside the house awaiting the commencement of the competition. Mia's plan is working! This will buy us some time before the bus arrives. (Where is that bus? Why are buses **always** running late?!)

Marjorie has gone full school principal mode and produced a **MEGAPHONE** to proclaim ...

THE ZOMBIE GAMES RULES

1. Always follow the rules or face immediate disqualification.

2. No eating fellow competitors' brains.

3. There will be various contests. ←

Keeping it vague but basically as many as we need until the bus gets here!

4. Points will be awarded to the winning side and the cumulative points tally will decide who gets the trophy.

5. Wash your hands before and after competing. (And maybe even during.) ←

Mum added this rule!

Incredibly, the zombies all seem to **GROAN** in agreement to abide by the rules. This thing is **ON!**

HUMANS VS
(AND DOG) 🐾

Dad is pumped!

Mia's family have joined us now

Yes, we are all wearing Marvelous Marvin merch. For team unity!

ELITE ATHLETE ZOMBIES

Maybe this wasn't such a good idea after all.

That's an intimidating show of strength

They are taking this seriously.

And there's heaps more behind them!

Check out the game faces!

'LET THE GAMES BEGIN!'

To pad out the time, we're commencing the proceedings with an opening ceremony, complete with **TORCH RELAY**. Anything to **DELAY** the games! Due to budget restraints (not to mention general zombie apocalypse supply chain issues) we are, however, working with a **BIRTHDAY CANDLE**.

By the time it reaches me the candle has **MELTED** away to a tiny little **STUB** ...

I fling the candle to the ground. Unfortunately the ground is covered in reams of **highly-flammable** toilet paper from the toilet paper torpedoes!

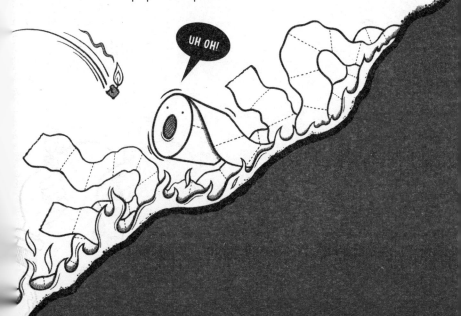

SQUIRT

Luckily Nan, and her hose, are never too far away and always ready to **SPRAY!** The fire is safely **extinguished**.

12:20pm

'LET THE GAMES BEGIN AGAIN!'

For insurance purposes we're skipping the torch ceremony this time round. We're not skipping **WARM UPS** though. Nan **INSISTS!** (Due to a few too many unfortunate incidents at her weekly Seniors' Aqua Aerobics Class.)

FLASHBACK

Nan takes the megaphone and leads us all through some ...

'WARM UPS!'

I follow Nan's directions.

Neck
stretches

Arm
stretches

Side
stretches

Leg
stretches

OK. That's me done.
I'm pooped. I'm off to
make a cup of tea.

No more delays. The zombies
are getting **impatient**. The air
is thick with anticipation ... or
maybe Dad just farted. Either
way **THE ZOMBIE GAMES** are
about to commence.

I've got a feeling these games are going to be worse than the worst sports day ever! And I've had some **doozies**.

FLASHBACKS

EXHIBIT A.
Not even making the sandpit in long jump

EXHIBIT B.
Going UNDER the bar at high jump

EXHIBIT C.
Sitting in the blazing sun ALL day bored out of my mind plucking grass after being eliminated in every single qualifying round for each event first thing in the morning.

1ST EVENT

HAMMER THROW

ZOMBIE GAMES RULES: Whoever throws furthest, wins!

Dad volunteers for the first event, and the zombies send forward their pick. Seems like a fair match up. **NOT!**

HAROLD CHASE
AKA: Poo Dad

STRENGTH ★★★★★
SPEED ♥♥♥♥♥
HEART ♥♥♥♥♥

VS

STATUS: HUMAN
RANKING: NUMBER 2 LOCAL PLUMBER (WALLY VALLEY AREA)

Special Skills: Farting on cue

Beard: Usually contains crumbs

THORN THORNINGTON
AKA: The Missile Launcher

STRENGTH ★★★★★★★
SPEED ♥♥♥♥♥
HEART ♥♥♥♥♥

STATUS: ZOMBIE
RANKING: FORMER HAMMER THROW WORLD CHAMPION

Special Skills: Throwing hammers

Beard: Majestic

The zombie goes first, spinning like a **TORNADO**, gathering the momentum to **FLING** the hammer into the **stratosphere**. Just before release though, the zombie gets **distracted** and the metal ball careens out of the official landing zone.

'HUH?'

Mum is enforcing the rules. (In her element!)

FOUL!

You can say that again. The **distraction** is **DAD!**

FOUL!

He's stripped down to his **birthday suit**. Apparently in honour of the ancient Olympians who competed **NUDE.**

Dad proudly **STRUTS** out in front of the crowd to the throwing circle. He licks his finger (FOUL!) and holds it in the air to gauge the wind direction. He gives his wrench a kiss (FOULER!) for **LUCK**. (He couldn't find his hammer so it's the closest compromise.)

And then he starts SPINNING, **BUCK NAKED!** (FOULEST!) **SO MUCH SPINNING AND NAKEDNESS!!**

Phew. At least the Poo Dad Plumbing tattoo WAS only temporary!*

WE NEED SOME SERIOUS PIXELLATION HERE! PLEASE!!

WON'T SOMEBODY THINK OF THE CHILDREN?

LOOK AWAY!

*See Worst Week Ever: Thursday page 33

SCENE DELETED

BY THE CENSORS

(MY EYES!)

PLease enjoy these adorabLe koaLa pictures instead . . .

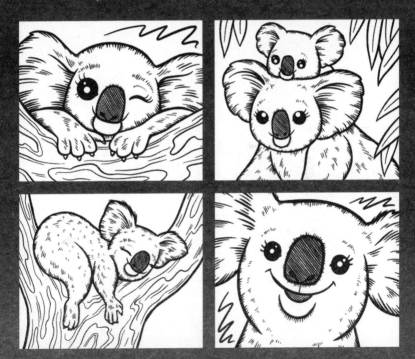

ApoLogies for the disruption to transmission.
We now resume our scheduled programming.

Aside from the gratuitous nudity, the throw is sheer perfection. The wrench sails through the air like a **COMET**.

'YAAAYYYY!'

Team Humans **ERUPTS** in a cheer. Miraculously, Dad has **WON** the hammer/wrench throw! It's official. We take the lead!

To celebrate, Dad does a victory lap. Unfortunately, for all of us, he's still **NAKED!**

SCENE DELETED

BY THE CENSORS
(SERIOUSLY. MY EYES!!!)

Please enjoy these cute baby giraffe pictures instead . . .

Apologies for the disruption to transmission.
We now resume our scheduled programming . . .

2ND EVENT
MIXED TEAM ARCHERY

ZOMBIE GAMES RULES: Highest team score, wins!

I'm teamed up with Mia. She does **archery** as a hobby.
I have a **HOPPY DOPPY** bow and arrow set. Perfect match!

MIA & JUSTIN
AKA: Team Straight and Arrow

STRENGTH ★★★★★
ACCURACY ●●●●●
HEART ♥♥♥♥♥

STRENGTH ★★★★★
ACCURACY ?????
HEART ♥♥♥♥♥

STATUS: HUMANS
RANKING: MIA - LOCAL AGE
CHAMPION. JUSTIN - UNKNOWN

Fun Fact: The Hoppy Doppy Bow & Arrow set was recalled for safety concerns

VS

HUNTER & BEAU
AKA: The Arch Enemies

STRENGTH ★★★★★
ACCURACY ●●●●●
HEART ♥♥♥♥♥

STRENGTH ★★★★★
ACCURACY ●●●●●
HEART ♥♥♥♥♥

STATUS: ZOMBIES
RANKING: FORMER MIXED TEAM
ARCHERY WORLD CHAMPIONS

Fun Fact: They never, ever, EVER miss

106

Zombie One **fires** their arrow with impeccable precision.

Mia **SHOOTS** her arrow, smooth and accurate.

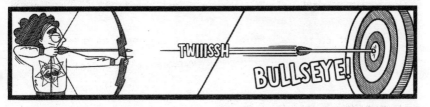

Zombie Two releases their arrow with robotic efficiency.

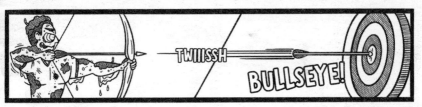

And now it's my turn! No pressure!

Not even on the board! I watch on, MORTIFIED,

as my arrow flies straight **OVER** the target ...

... and ricochets around the yard ...

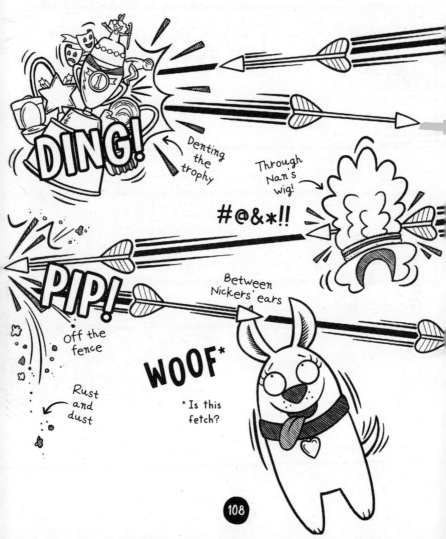

ZING!

DING!

Denting the trophy

Through Nan's wig!

#@&*!!

PIP!

off the fence

Rust and dust

Between Nickers' ears

WOOF*

* Is this fetch?

108

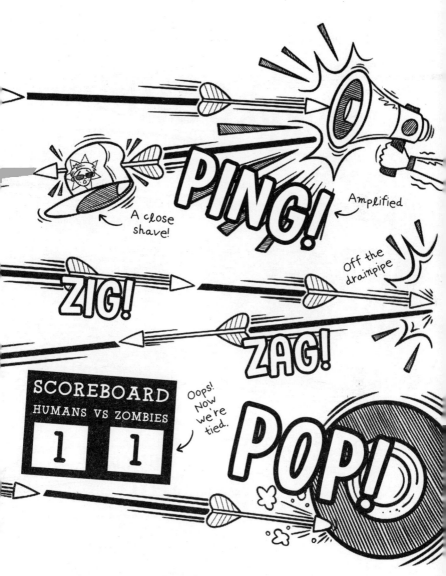

... until it pierces straight into the front tyre of ...

... the Wally Valley Hustle Bustle bus that has just driven onto the scene.

AAARRRGGHH!

There's some familiar unexpected passengers too!

CAUTION

CAUTION

DO NOT CROSS   DO NOT CROSS   DO

ZOMBIE APOCALYPSE IN PROGRESS   ZOMBIE APOCALYPSE IN PROGRESS

1 SP33D

SCREEEECH!

It's a total tyre **BLOWOUT!** The bus SWERVES out of control, **skidding** across the yard, heading straight at ME!

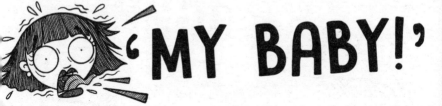

'MY BABY!'

The bus driver frantically **SPINS** the steering wheel. Now the bus is heading straight for Dad's **toilet truck.**

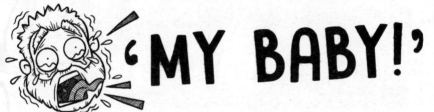

'MY BABY!'

A collision is **inevitable!** The driver and passengers LEAP from the bus to **safety** (a relative term considering they're landing in a yard filled with zombies!) and then ...

BEFORE

AFTER

Luckily, no-one was hurt. On the downside though, the bus that was meant to save us has been **TOTALLED** and also **DESTROYED** our only other possible means of vehicular ESCAPE from the elite athlete zombies. DANG!

The bus driver remains unfazed and optimistic in the face of our current adversity.

Meanwhile, our team has some notable new additions thanks to the Wally Valley Hustle Bustle Special School Bookings Policy: **NO STAFF LEFT BEHIND!** Usually that applies specifically to zoo visits (due to a previous **incident** with Mr Majors and the gorilla enclosure) but also, apparently, zombie apocalypse evacuations. So we are now joined by a few of Wally Valley Public School's finest ...

NEW RECRUITS

MR MAJORS – Year 6 teacher
(currently on personal leave)

Useful skill set: Yelling, clipboard carrying and whistle blowing

TOOOT!

SUCH TEAM SPIRIT!

WORST GAMES EVER

10 0

MISS DENISE and MISS BERNICE – Front Office Ladies

Useful skill set: Officiating and judging

MR DEWEY – School Librarian

Useful skill set: The wisdom of books

I'll just be over here reading.

3RD EVENT
FOOTBALL

ZOMBIE GAMES RULES: Five a side. Most goals wins

We've picked a football match next to buy as much time as possible for bus/truck repairs.

MARVIN'S MARVELS
AKA: The Drop Kicks

VS

THE GOATs
AKA: The Greatest Of All Time

STATUS: HUMAN & CANINE
RANKING: UNRANKED, UNKEMPT, UNPREPARED UNDER DOGS

STATUS: ZOMBIES
RANKING: FORMER FOOTBALL SUPERSTAR WORLD CHAMPIONS

Special Note: I voted AGAINST the team name but Marvin insisted

Special Note: A league of legendary Hat Trick Heroes

The football superstars ANNIHILATE us in the first half.

We are outplayed and **outclassed**. The zombies are ...

There's ...
FEINTING

and ... **HEADING**

and consequently ...
BE-HEADING

and subsequently ...
FAINTING!

And there is ...   after ...   after ...

GOAL! GOAL! GOAL!

... as our side stands there like **STUNNED MULLETS.**

1:45pm

HALFTIME! Finally, we can get a short break from our humiliating on-field **domination.** We skip the traditional **SNACK** of orange quarters (as we don't want the zombies thinking about **brain** halves!) and move straight on to the motivational speech. Some encouraging, **positive** words would be helpful right about now. Bring on the **PEP TALK** ...

Make that **pep-SHOUT!** Mr Majors has decided to **inspire** the team.

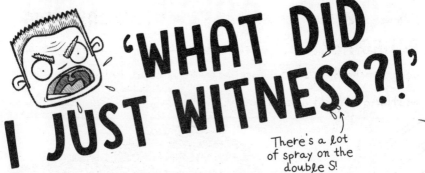

'WHAT DID I JUST WITNESS?!'

There's a lot of spray on the double S!

I go to answer (A: 'Possibly the first **ever** humans plus dog versus zombies five-a-side football match') but then realise that was one of those **RHETORICAL** questions teachers **love** to ask. Which is very confusing because they ask a lot of non-rhetorical questions too and, really, how am I supposed to know which is which? (That wasn't a rhetorical question, by the way.)

Mr Majors continues his **pep-TIRADE**.

'YOU'RE AN EMBARRASSMENT TO THE LIVING! YOU'RE BEING BEATEN BY LITERAL DEAD PEOPLE. I HAVE BACK PIMPLES WITH MORE GUTS THAN YOU! I HAVE INGROWN NOSE HAIRS WITH MORE DETERMINATION THAN YOU! NOW GET BACK OUT THERE AND SHOW ME WHAT YOU'VE GOT!'

It's the second half, and Marvin, always the teacher's pet, follows directions and shows us what he's got ... **AMAZING ACTING ABILITIES!** When one of the zombie players brushes past him he **THROWS** himself to the ground and starts writhing around dramatically.

> **MY LEG!**
>
> **OH, THE UNBEARABLE AGONY.**
>
> **WILL I EVER WALK AGAIN?**

And what a performance! I can see another amateur theatre acting gong being awarded for this.

FLASH FORWARD

Best Actor: **MARVIN KING** in 'THE DIVE'

Thank you, fans! Some of my finest work

We're also **awarded** a free **PENALTY** kick!

But **WHO** will take the free kick?

Marvin is still **FLAILING** around on the ground like a cockroach just squirted with insect spray.

Wish I had Anti-Marvin spray in real life!

Mia and her brother, Carlos, don't usually play football so they don't volunteer. And Nickers is ... digging a hole.

So it looks like it's up to **ME** to take the penalty shot.

THE PRESSURE!

I'm sweating **BUCKETS**. My stomach is **CHURNING**.

It's a whirlpool in there

SWEAT DIRECT FROM THE PITS

ICK!

I'm having **FLASHBACKS!** **FLASHBACKS!** **FLASHBACKS!**

to my many, **many** past missed goals. But I have to **FOCUS**.

I can't let my team down, even if my team is called

MARVIN'S MARVELS.

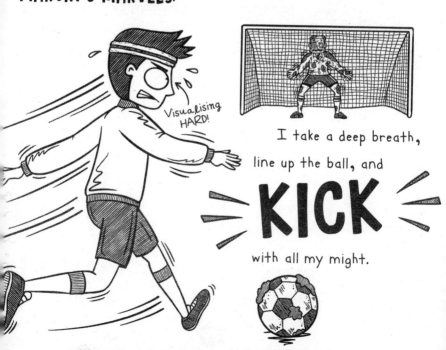

Visualising HARD!

I take a deep breath,

line up the ball, and

KICK

with all my might.

Time seems to **SLOW** down as I watch the ball **HURTLE** towards the goal.

WHOOOSSHH!

I cross my fingers.	And my **TOES**.	And my **LEGS**.	And even my eyes!

The ball is right on track! For a second I'm **HOPEFUL**, but then the zombie goalkeeper moves directly into its path.

Correction. The ball goes straight **THROUGH** the goalie! Like a **CANNONBALL!** It hits the back of the net. It's officially a ...

We are **finally** on the board for this football match. OK, we're still losing but at least we have **ONE** point!

1 VS 97

I don't know what overcomes me, but I start doing **celebratory** dance moves. **DAD'S** dance moves.

THE LAWNMOWER

THE SPRINKLER

CH-CH-CH-CH-CH

THE FLOSS

THAT'S MY BOY!

And then I pull my top over my head and **run** around in circles. I can't stop myself! I'm **ELATED!**

Until I run into the side of the house ...

THUNK!

'OOOPH!'

I'm fine. All good. Nothing to see here. Let's move on.

`2:13pm`

Play **resumes** and **The GOATs** are whipping us again, until Nickers **INTERCEPTS!** Of course Nickers is able to steal the ball. **STEALING** is her super power.

Nickers is heading for the **GOAL!**

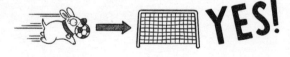 **YES!**

Nickers is heading **PAST** the goal.

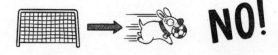 **NO!**

Nickers is heading into the **cemetery!**

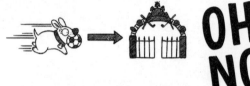 **OH NO!**

Not this again!

Hey, kids! (And zombies!!)
It's BACK and even better than before.
If you loved playing GET THOSE DOGGONE
SHORTS then get hyped for ...

EXCLUSIVE TO CFEA*

* Cemetery For
Elite Athletes

I didn't like this game the first time[*] and I like it even LESS now that:

1. it is **MULTIPLAYER** (and the other players are elite athlete ZOMBIES.)

2. the creepy **cemetery** is **ALIVE** with fresh zombies breaking out of the ground everywhere.

I'm not just dodging **headstones** this time. ➔

I'm having to avoid scary, grabby zombie hands. ➔

I'm tripping and **STUMBLING** and I can't keep up with the zombies who are chasing Nickers for the ball, too. I'm fast in the pool, but on land I've got nothing!

(Except at night when I **SPRINT** from the light switch to my bed when I turn off the lights, **racing** to get safely beneath the covers before whatever is LURKING under my bed can emerge in the darkness. **THEN** I'm fast.)

New land speed record?

*See *Worst Week Ever: Tuesday* page 63

I watch on in **AWE**. The zombies are like graceful **gazelles** bounding over the headstones in their path. Somehow the football match has **MORPHED** into …

A SURPRISE UNSCHEDULED EVENT
HURDLES

ZOMBIE GAMES RULES: Jump over all the headstones

That **competitive spirit** has kicked in and the zombies have lost interest in Nickers and now seem more focussed on racing each other, clearing the headstones at impressive speed. And, this being a cemetery, there are a **LOT** of headstones. The graves stretch to the horizon and soon the zombies have **HURDLED** off into the distance.

Now I have to catch Nickers. And I do catch her! I **bust** Nickers digging another one of her holes. Not just any hole. I've found her stash of special buried **TREASURE!**

WOOF*

* Ahoy there!

There's so many 'missing' items in the hole. Notably a **LOT** of souvenirs from the **Toilet Appreciation Museum.** Dad's going to be so relieved. There may be ugly crying!

They were out of HARRY'S

LARRY'S

T.A.M.

MY DAD WENT TO THE TOILET APPRECIATION MUSEUM AND ALL I GOT WAS THIS LOUSY T-SHIRT

Dad's keyring   Nan's teapot   My T-shirt

Right at the bottom of the hole though is the mysterious island **TALISMAN** Nickers nicked from me on Thursday.

I reach in and grab the strange object, brushing away the soil. It's **glowing** iridescent blue, just like the zombies, and is oddly warm to touch, like one of Nan's biscuits fresh from the oven.

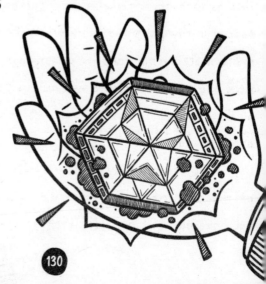

At the same time I notice a nearby zombie hand **stops** **CLAWING** its way out of the dirt and **retreats** peacefully back underground.

GOING ...   GOING ...   GONE!

Have I just somehow **STOPPED** the zombie apocalypse Nickers inadvertently started? Is this curious **CHARM** cupped in my palm the cause of it all? Why am I now being menacingly **surrounded** by a congregation of **CATS?** And why were the zombie athletes all nonsensically (yet conveniently, plot-wise) buried wearing their sporting uniforms **WITH** their athletic equipment?

There are so many questions **WHIRLING** through my head at this moment. And there's one person you can trust when you have big **QUESTIONS** that need **ANSWERS** ...

No, definitely **NOT** Dad!

It was the Mole People working together with the dolphins! We're doomed!

I meant ...

A LIBRARIAN!

2:33pm

I track down Mr Dewey and show him the TALISMAN. His eyes go **WIDE**. 'That's a **fascinating** find, young man!'

He examines the shiny object, slowly turning it over, holding it up to the light, and muttering to himself. 'Interesting ... Hmmmm ... Peculiar ... Tut. Tut. Tut. ... Golly ... I wonder?'

White glove

'**WHAT IS IT?**' I impatiently interrupt.

You used the word 'talisman', which is impressive. Great vocabulary! And indeed it does have the appearance of one.

Oh, no. I just wanted a quick answer and he's launched into the extended edition.

Many civilisations believed talismans – mystical objects – possessed magical powers linked to the astrological, spiritual or supernatural.

Groan! This is like school. On a SATURDAY!

Intriguingly, there appears to be the face of a cat carved into its surface. Fun fact: some ancient cultures worshipped cats!

Wait! How did I not notice the cat face?!

Though I'm not sure what it is made out of. And I can recite the periodic table of elements, alphabetically AND backwards. It's my party trick!

Mental note: Don't invite Mr Dewey to my next birthday party.

This may well be a priceless artefact of huge historical and cultural significance or, then again, it might be a piece of cheap junk from the two dollar shop. Hard to say without the proper research.

Let's wind this up. The hurdling zombies are almost back!

So in answer to your question, 'What is it?' well ...

I have no idea!

But I do have some books you might find interesting!

How do librarians always have the perfect books on hand? Even in the middle of a zombie apocalypse!

2:45pm

There's no time to tackle my new **TBR*** pile. The full time whistle has been blown on the football match (Team Zombies wins) and the hurdlers are back (another point their way).

SCOREBOARD
HUMANS VS ZOMBIES
1 **3**

And, even though new zombies have stopped popping up out of the ground, we still have a whole existing **squad** of zombies eager to either eat our brains (bad!) or compete (preferable!). We need to come up with **MORE** sporting distractions!

I have some books that might help!

He's done it again!

* To Be Read

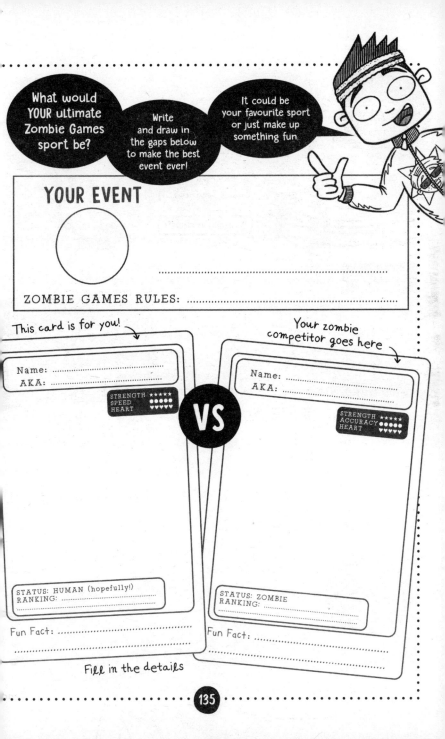

What would YOUR ultimate Zombie Games sport be?

Write and draw in the gaps below to make the best event ever!

It could be your favourite sport or just make up something fun.

YOUR EVENT

ZOMBIE GAMES RULES: ....

This card is for you!

Name: ....
AKA: ....

STRENGTH ★★★★★
SPEED ●●●●●
HEART ♥♥♥♥♥

VS

Your zombie competitor goes here

Name: ....
AKA: ....

STRENGTH ★★★★★
ACCURACY ●●●●●
HEART ♥♥♥♥♥

STATUS: HUMAN (hopefully!)
RANKING: ....

STATUS: ZOMBIE
RANKING: ....

Fun Fact: ....

Fun Fact: ....

Fill in the details

135

3:00pm

5TH EVENT

SUMO WRESTLING

ZOMBIE GAMES RULES: Force opponent down or out of the ring

Dad volunteered for this one. Any excuse to **strip** down again! However, now it's time to fight, he's **VANISHED!**

HAROLD CHASE
AKA: M.I.A

STRENGTH ★★★★★
SPEED ●●●●●
HEART ♥♥♥♥♥

MISSING

STATUS: HUMAN
RANKING: NUMBER 1... FAN OF THE MIGHTY FERRETS

Hair: Thinning on top
Appearance: Invisible

VS

YAMA TSUNAMI
AKA: The Mountain Masher

STRENGTH ★★★★★
SPEED ●●●●●
HEART ♥♥♥♥♥

STATUS: ZOMBIE
RANKING: FORMER SUMO GRAND CHAMPION

Hair: Impressive top knot
Appearance: Intimidating

Dad didn't **chicken** out though. He **FERRETED** out!

LESS THIS   **MORE THAT**

Pecky the Chook

Freddy the Ferret

When he spotted the zombie former captain of the original premiership team of his favourite Australian football club, The Mighty Ferrets, Dad went **WILD**. Now, instead of getting chased by a zombie, Dad is chasing after one of them. For an autograph. In his undies. With the crazed **FERVOUR** of a Chaser chasing T.H.E. Justin Chase.

Happy tears!

I LOVE YOU! WILL YOU SIGN MY TUMMY?

The tables have turned!

Which leaves us facing a **TOWERING** sumo-wrestler zombie who is getting very **IMPATIENT**, waiting for an opponent to enter the ring (AKA Nan's hose in a circle). We need a **competitor** quickly!

'I'll do it!' Marvin surprises me by stepping forward. 'Except I'm still tragically injured from football so I nominate **Justin** instead.' And then he pushes me into the ring.

Looks like the sumo match is now ...

JUSTIN CHASE
AKA: Slim Chance

STRENGTH ★★★★★
SPEED ●●●●●
HEART ♥♥♥♥♥

Nervous gas

STATUS: HUMAN
RANKING: IS NEGATIVE RANKING A THING?

Prediction: About to be turned into pancakes

VS

YAMA TSUNAMI
AKA: The Justin Exterminator

STRENGTH ★★★★★
SPEED ●●●●●
HEART ♥♥♥♥♥

STATUS: ZOMBIE
RANKING: FORMER SUMO GRAND CHAMPION

Prediction: About to make pancakes

I try to protest that this is **NOT** a fair fight but Marvin points out there are no weight divisions in sumo wrestling.

Rules are rules, Poo Boy!

Enough with the books now, Mr Dewey!!

So the match **BEGINS!**

Which is kind of like a wind-up **bunny** versus a **T-REX**.

Or a delicate **goldfish** versus a savage **SHARK**.

Or a little kid,
i.e. ME, versus a
gargantuan **ZOMBIE
SUMO WRESTLER!**

There is **no** competition. All I can really do is **RUN** in
circles around the ring trying to **EVADE** the zombie's grasp.
I'm like a time-lapse of a tiny moon orbiting a giant planet.

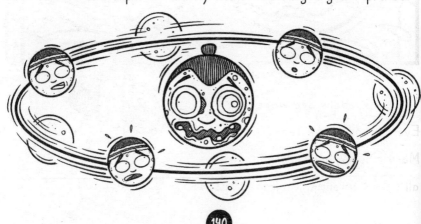

But, inevitably, the zombie grabs me!

More specifically, they grab the waistband of my not-so-lucky, back-up, back-up **UNDIES**, while my momentum is still PROPELLING my body forwards, which means ...

WEDGIE!

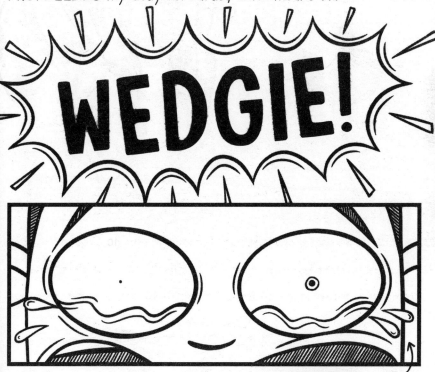

My eyeballs are **watering**! Even through the tears I can see Marvin is joyfully recording this all on his infernal tablet.

NOT happy tears!

Quality content! Livestreaming now!

I feel a fresh **ANGER** rise up inside of me, giving me renewed energy. I **WRITHE** and **WRIGGLE** free, then revert back to running rings around the wrestler.

I actually think my strategy might be working. The zombie is getting **DIZZY!**

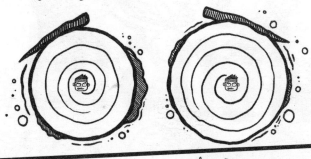

They're losing their **BALANCE.** Their tree trunk legs are **WOBBLING.**

YES!

They're slowly falling backwards ... towards **ME!**

NO!

If I was in a forest now I'd be yelling:

'TIMBER!'

6TH EVENT
RHYTHMIC GYMNASTICS

ZOMBIE GAMES APPARATUS: Ribbon

Wasn't expecting to see my school principal/new step-mum in a **twirl off** against a zombie today, but here we are.

MARJORIE KING-CHASE
AKA: The Principal

STRENGTH ★★★★☆
GRACE ♥♥♥♥♥
HEART

STATUS: HUMAN
RANKING: MISS WALLY VALLEY
RUNNER UP, 5 YEARS IN A ROW

Special Skills: Good at giving Detention
Signature Move: Spirit fingers

VS

TWIRLY TWISTER
AKA: The Human Hurricane

STRENGTH ★★★★★
GRACE ♥♥♥♥♥
HEART

STATUS: ZOMBIE
RANKING: FORMER GYMNASTICS
GOLD MEDALIST

Special Skills: Good at getting attention
Signature Move: Super spiral

Hypnotic

The zombie gymnast executes a **flawless** routine. (Yet Miss Bernice **STILL** manages to find a flaw.)

SPIN-TACULAR! SHEER PERFECTION!

LOST 2 POINTS FOR DROOLING!

10 8

JUDGES' COMMENTS

Marjorie starts off well, **DAZZLING** with her mastery of the ribbon/toilet paper and her **bedazzled** swimsuit ...

THAT'S MY WIFE!

... but things unfortunately take a turn for the worse. It's a downward **SPIRAL** as Marjorie **SPINS** out of control and ends up **swaddled** in three-ply.

MUMMY!

Hip knotted

POETRY IN MOTION! BEAUTIFULLY WRAPPED.

DERIVATIVE. THAT'S A WASTE OF GOOD TOILET PAPER!

10 -1

JUDGES' COMMENTS

It's a **WIPEOUT!**
Team Zombies win **again!**

SCOREBOARD
HUMANS VS ZOMBIES

1   5

7TH EVENT

TABLE TENNIS

ZOMBIE GAMES RULES: First to 21 points wins

Time for Vlad to **bat.** (Not vampire bat unfortunately.)
He's going to put those lightning-fast **reflexes** to good use.

VLADIMIR STOKER
AKA: Step-Vlad

STRENGTH ★★★★★
SPEED ●●●●●
HEART ?????

STATUS: HUMAN? VAMPIRE?
RANKING: PRINCE OF DARKNESS?
SECOND HUSBAND.

Special Skills: Dampening the mood

Signature Move: Lurk

VS

FLIP LONG
AKA: King Ping Pong

STRENGTH ★★★★★
SPEED ●●●●●
HEART ●●●●●

STATUS: ZOMBIE
RANKING: FORMER TABLE
TENNIS WORLD CHAMPION

Special Skills: Fun at parties

Signature Move: Smash

The ball is a **BLUR** as it FLIES back and forth between their paddles. The speed and intensity is amazing, but Vlad isn't even breaking a sweat. (Probably because vampires don't sweat. Even **MORE** irrefutable vampire proof!)

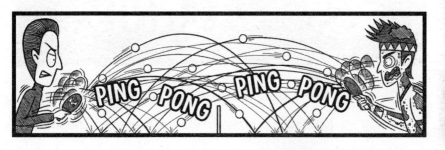

It's **MESMERISING!** My head is **swivelling** so fast following the ball my brain must be SHAKEN. I find myself actually **cheering** for Vlad as the game goes on.

THAT'S MY STEP-DAD!

The zombie goes for a powerful ...

SMASH!

Vlad instantly returns it with equal FORCE.

WHACK!

Straight into the zombie's FACE.

BEFORE

Incoming Ball

AFTER

Outgoing Eyeball

And now, somehow, they're playing with an **EYEBALL!**
Which is a bit less bouncy and a lot more SMOOSHY.

With the advantage of **both** eyes, Vlad eventually wins the epic match. Go Humans! (And, possibly, vampires!)

SCOREBOARD
HUMANS VS ZOMBIES
2   5

5:00pm

8TH EVENT
COMPETITIVE EATING

ZOMBIE GAMES RULES: Eat the most, the fastest

Mr Majors steps up to the table. If this was a **chocolate** eating competition I would have happily volunteered. But it's only **HOT DOGS** on the menu today.

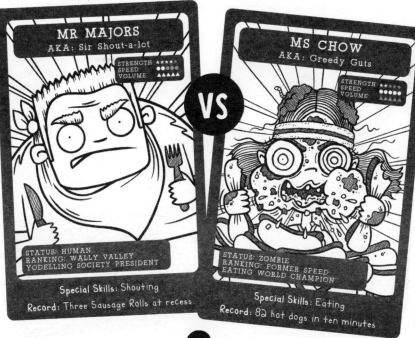

MR MAJORS
AKA: Sir Shout-a-lot

STRENGTH ★★★★☆
SPEED ●●●●○
VOLUME ▲▲▲▲▲

STATUS: HUMAN
RANKING: WALLY VALLEY
YODELLING SOCIETY PRESIDENT

Special Skills: Shouting
Record: Three Sausage Rolls at recess

VS

MS CHOW
AKA: Greedy Guts

STRENGTH ★★★★★
SPEED ●●●●●
VOLUME ▲▲▲☆☆

STATUS: ZOMBIE
RANKING: FORMER SPEED
EATING WORLD CHAMPION

Special Skills: Eating
Record: 82 hot dogs in ten minutes

Dad is in charge of food prep, so these **aren't** your regular delicious **hot dogs**.

LESS LIKE THIS

MORE LIKE THAT

He's cooked up some **disgusting** green beans and broccoli faux frankfurters (boiled!), topped with brussels sprouts sauce and served in leftover dinner rolls from Thursday's wedding (which are looking pretty **mouldy** by now).

Plates piled with **PUTRID** hot dogs are placed in front of Mr Majors and his competitor. The **EAT OFF** begins!

It starts fast with them both **SCOFFING** the 'food' down at an impressive pace. The stacks of hot dogs are quickly **WHITTLED** away.

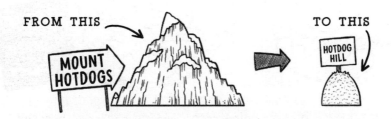

FROM THIS

MOUNT HOTDOGS

TO THIS

HOTDOG HILL

Then I notice Mr Majors is starting to slow down. There are some telltale signs of **TROUBLE**.

His eyes are bulging.

Sweat is dripping from his forehead

His puffed cheeks, crammed to capacity, are no longer moving from chewing.

Each attempt to swallow is failing

The hot dogs no longer want to go **down**. In fact, the hot dogs want to come **UP**. In a HURRY!

SCENE DELETED

BY THE CENSORS

(IMAGINE SPEED EATING GREEN HOT DOGS... IN REVERSE!)

Please enjoy these cute baby mouse lemur pictures instead ...

Apologies for the disruption to transmission.
We now resume our scheduled programming ...

GREEN going in and **GREEN** going out! Mr Majors is **disqualified** and the zombies take the point. And Nan has some serious hosing down to do.

We check in on the escape vehicle repairs. In the grand tradition of most buses, it is running **behind** schedule.

We still need to buy more time. The games must go on!

We're getting **desperate,** and really pushing the limits of credible plausibility, but the zombies actually don't seem to mind what the sport is. As long as they're COMPETING, they're **not** eating!

NEXT ZOMBIE GAMES EVENTS

5:30 pm	SKATEBOARDING
6:00 pm	FENCING
6:30 pm	RUNNING OF THE BULLS
6:32 pm	CROQUET
7:00 pm	LOG ROLLING
7:30 pm	MINI GOLF
8:00 pm	RODEO BULL RIDING
8:01 pm	ROLLER DERBY
8:30 pm	DODGE BALL

Mia's bro, Carlos, has the best moves. He's so cool! ←

That was fast! ←

I got a hole in one! ←

That was faster! ←

Marvin keeps hitting ME. And we're on the same team. Very dodgy! ←

We've made an impressive **comeback** on the tally board! Now that we actually have a chance of winning I'm starting to enjoy the **ZOMBIE GAMES!**

SCOREBOARD
HUMANS VS ZOMBIES
8   9

9:00pm

18TH EVENT

ARM WRESTLING

ZOMBIE GAMES RULES: Pin your opponent's hand down

Mum could be the one to even the score! I've warned you before. She's tiny, but do **NOT** mess with this lady!

ANGELICA MARY-GRACE JOY MANALO DELA-CRUZ STOKER
AKA: Yes, Mum

STRENGTH ★★★★★
SPEED ●●●●●
HEART ♥♥♥♥♥

VS

RIP BRAWN
AKA: Arm-ageddon

STRENGTH ★★★★★
SPEED ●●●●●
HEART ♥♥♥♥♥

FLEX

STATUS: HUMAN
RANKING: TOO MANY TO LIST.
BEST HUGGER EVER.

Special Skills: Crushing insubordinance with raised eyebrow

KISS

STATUS: ZOMBIE
RANKING: FORMER ARM WRESTLING WORLD CHAMPION

Special Skills: Crushing metal cans with bare hands

The arm wrestle begins and the zombie appears surprised when Mum is able to hold her ground against their force. They're even more **surprised** when Mum unleashes her SECRET WEAPON. No. Not laser eyes. A barrage of constant **DISAPPOINTMENT!**

The zombie is taken aback by the questioning (**Amateur!** They should have **ZONED** out like I do!) With their focus broken Mum is able to **snap** the zombie's arm down onto the table. And when I say **SNAP**, I mean **SNAP**. The zombie's arm comes clean **OFF!** Which takes us to a tie ...

19TH EVENT

TUG OF WAR

ZOMBIE GAMES RULES: Out-pull the other team

It's all hands on deck. Or rather **rope**. Or, more specifically, Nan's garden **HOSE**, for a tie-breaking **TUG OF WAR** match.

TEAM HUMANS
AKA: All of us

STRENGTH ★★★★
STAMINA ♥♥♥♥
GRUNT

So over Marvin's face!

STATUS: HUMANS
RANKING: THE UNLUCKIEST PEOPLE ON THE PLANET?

Motto: Get a grip!
Status: At the end of our rope

VS

TEAM ZOMBIES
AKA: All of them

STRENGTH ★★★★★
STAMINA ♥♥♥♥♥
GRUNT

STATUS: ZOMBIE
RANKING: THE MOST ELITE ATHLETES TO EVER LIVE (TWICE)

Motto: TROPHY!/BRAINS!
Status: Impressive pulling power

HEAVE PULL

H H H H H H H H
- - - - - - - - - - - - -
H H H H H H H H

It's not looking good for Team Humans. We're getting dragged by the zombies.

GRUNT STRAIN

H H H H H H H H H
- - - - - - - - - - - - -
H H H H H H H H H

Any second now and we're going right over the gutter onto the next page!

PANT SWEAT

H H H H H H H H H
- - - - - - - - - - - - -
H H H H H H H H H

B — Oi! The bus is ready!

'FINALLY!'

H H H H H H H H
H H H H H H H H

MOAN GROAN

ZZZZZZZZ

ZZZZZZZZ

MOAN GROAN

ZZZZZZZZ

ZZZZZZZZ

MOAN GROAN

ZZZZZZZZ

ZZZZZZZZ

GROOOAN!

We let go of the hose and watch the zombies going **FLYING** backwards ...

ZZZZZZZZ

ZZZZZZZZ

... straight into the GIANT **SINKHOLE** that is, luckily for us, **unluckily** for them and **conveniently** for the plot, right behind them!

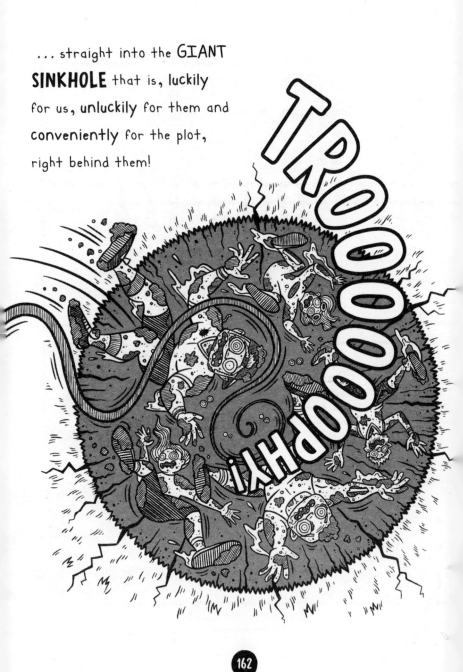

Technically we didn't win, as it's against the rules to let go of the rope (or even hose) in tug of war, **BUT** all of the zombies are now in a big hole so it is kind of a **VICTORY!**

GO TEAM HUMANS! We did it! There's so many ...

FIST BUMPS,   HIGH FIVES   AND HUGS!

The celebrations are interrupted by the loud **revving** of an engine. Our **getaway** vehicle is unveiled and ready to roll.

All aboard ...

GET ON, PEEPS! IT'S GO TIME!

NEXT STOP: WALLY HEIGHTS!

We all **clamber** up into the bus/truck **MONSTROSITY** and take off, leaving the Cemetery for Elite Athletes and The Zombie Games in a cloud of smoke. Now we just have to make it up the steep mountain to Princess's high-security **mansion**. **NOTHING** can stop us. Except maybe the spluttering engine, gravity or possibly ...

... some very **persistent** zombies who are chasing after us. On **BIKES!**

ZOMBIKES!

Typical elite athletes and their refusal to ever give up!

Uphill too! I always have to get off my bike and walk it, even for a slight slope.

Dad tries to **BLAST** the zombies off their bicycles with the water cannon, but it does nothing!

It's shower time!

FWOOOSH

The driver is now steering the bus **erratically** from side to side. Although I'm not sure if she is even trying to **EVADE** the zombies, or that's just her **standard** driving style!

The **BUS/TRUCK** is SWERVING wildly on the road, but we just can't **SHAKE** those tenacious, lycra-clad zombies. However, it does seem to be **SHAKING** the remaining green hot dogs SLOSHING around in Mr Majors' stomach. He's not looking good! The **chaotic** ride is eventually too much. He lunges for the window and lets fly with a spray of vivid green **SPEW**.

FROM THIS

TO THIS

Better out than in.

At least the other windows are closed this time!

SCENE DELETED

BY THE CENSORS
(SPEEEEEEEEEEEEEEEEEW!)

Please enjoy these sweet, fluffy chinchilla pictures instead...

Apologies for the disruption to transmission.
We now resume our scheduled programming...

The **slick** of slimy sick on the road makes all the bikes ...

We leave the **pile-up** of zombikes in the rear-view mirror as we **SPEED** on to the safety of the **high-security** mansion.

10:03pm

Unfortunately we can't get past the **high-security** at the mansion! We're **BLOCKED** by an imposing gate while being intimidated by laser beams and circled by threatening drones.

We climb out of the bus/truck and cautiously **tiptoe** over to the **video intercom**.

There's a momentary pause and then an ear-piercing ...

SHRIIIIIEK!

Princess appears on the screen. But her face soon goes ...

FROM THIS

TO THIS

'Ewwww! It's only you!' Princess doesn't even try to hide her **DISAPPOINTMENT.**

'Princess! You've gotta let us in. Please! There's ...'

'**ZOMBIES.** I know! I've been watching **The Zombie Games** all day, along with the rest of the world. It's all anyone's talking about online.'

'Hey! That's **MY** footage, from **MY** channel!' Marvin is **OUTRAGED.**

Princess groans. 'Correction. **MY** Daddy **OWNS** the platform your channel is on and anything you upload so it's **HIS** footage now. Read the **fine print,** loser! Anyway, if there's no actual Justin Chase I'm going ...'

'Wait, Princess. Please. Let us in!' I beg.

Princess is deliberating. 'Well, I suppose on the pro side, I could get some internet **CLOUT,** saving **Team Humans.** On the con side, though, you're all **GROSS,** and clearly from a lower socio-economic group **AND** covered in zombie **SLIME.**'

'I'll give you Justin Chase's phone number!' I bargain.

'**DEAL!** Come in, but no touching the artworks!'

As soon as I hand over the phone number, the giant automated gates begin to slide OPEN! Nickers is the first through the gap, and straight to **butt-sniffing**. Can't take her anywhere!

* You truly are a thief, because you've stolen my heart!
** Oh, behave, you smooth-talking Short King!

Everyone else files through the gate and then it slowly begins to slide close. We're finally **SAFE!** And then I remember the **Ultimate Super Duper Mega Trophy** is tucked under my seat back on the truck/bus. I can't leave it behind now! (I'm still hoping to salvage my beloved swimming trophies after all this.)

I dart back and grab it. But something **GRABS** me. Around the ankle. It's the snapped-off ZOMBIE ARM!

I hobble back towards the gate but it is ... closing ... CLOSING ... **CLOSED!**

OPEN THE GATE!

THERE'S A TIME LOCK DELAY BEFORE IT CAN OPEN AGAIN!

So everyone else is on **that** side of the gate, while I'm on **THIS** side with the angry zombie arm. I am literally arm wrestling, and definitely **LOSING**.

Ewww! Zombie Wet Willy.

Until I recall the **motivating** force of all elite athlete zombies. I loudly announce in my most official voice: 'I challenge you, Zombie Arm, to the tie-breaking event to decide the overall Zombie Games **WINNER** and who gets the **TROPHY**. Let's play ... '

FINAL EVENT

ROCK, PAPER, SCISSORS

ZOMBIE GAMES RULES: You know the rules!

My fingers are limber and fit from all that **secret handshake** practice earlier in the week. I've got this!

JUSTIN CHASE
AKA: Justickles Fingerkles

ROCK
PAPER
SCISSORS

STATUS: HUMAN
RANKING: TWO THUMBS UP

Status: Seasoned finger-puller

VS

JUST AN ARM
AKA: Hand Solo

ROCK
PAPER
SCISSORS

STATUS: ZOMBIE
RANKING: JUST ONE THUMB UP

Status: Quite handy

Whatever the zombie arm throws down I'm magically **matching**. We're perfectly in **SYNC!**

We keep on going ...

As the match **DRAGS** on in a never-ending **stalemate** it begins to dawn on me that I don't need to win. When I look up to see the gate is finally opening, the **REAL PRIZE** is revealed. Mum. Dad. Nan. Nickers. Mia. Even Vlad and Marjorie. (I can take or leave Marvin! Preferably, leave.)

I sense the zombie arm is about to throw down 'PAPER' so I **'ROCK'**.

 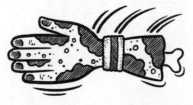

I'm **BEATEN.** The zombies have officially **WON** the Zombie Games. It's over!

The zombie arm does an **obnoxious** victory dance and snatches up the **TROPHY,** leaving me to run to my family and friends for a **BIG ...**

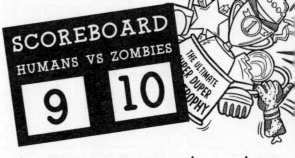

SCOREBOARD
HUMANS VS ZOMBIES
9 | 10

THE ULTIMATE SUPER DUPER TROPHY

GROUP HUG!

KA-CHING!   KA-CHING!

The hug is interrupted by my phone in my pocket, ringing. Which is when Princess realises that I've given her **MY** phone number (which **IS** technically A Justin Chase's phone number).

10:15 – 10:46pm

'WHAAH!'

10:47pm

When the **TANTRUM** finally subsides, Princess is thankfully bored enough (her mum's asleep and her dad's away on business) to let us temporarily stay in the mansion. On the condition we do the latest viral dance for her social media (groan!) **AND** get cleaned up and changed (with pleasure!).

The only spare clothes she has for us all are **T.H.E.** Justin Chase merchandise, which is 178% better than Marvelous Marvin merch!

FROM THIS   **TO THIS**

← Zombie juice

My signature!

177

I'm so happy we all survived a **ZOMBIE APOCALYPSE**.

I'm less happy the ZOMBIE GAMES are now being replayed

on repeat and we're all watching it together on Princess's

home theatre big screen. (And when you're the daughter of

a **BILLIONAIRE**, a **big** screen is actually a **HUGE** screen.)

Reliving a zombie **wedgie** in high definition, and surround sound

at ten times the size, is a hundred times more **MORTIFYING**.

It's a **relief** when the television broadcast suddenly cuts

out and the screen turns to crackling **static**. Finally I'm

having some GOOD LUCK.

Or maybe **not**! The **STATIC** is clearing and a familiar face is emerging.

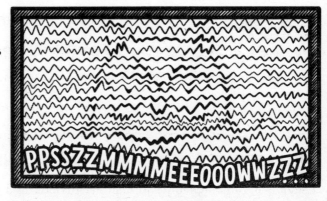

Is that my beloved, missing pet cat inexplicably turning up on the TV ... **AGAIN?!**

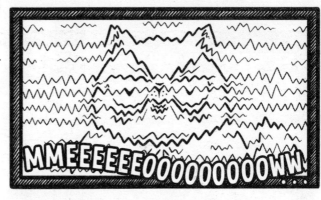

It is! He's back. It's **CAPTAIN FLUFFYKINS** evil laughing on the screen!

And this time I actually have **witnesses!** Who now all look like they wish they had a big drink to SPIT out in **SHOCK!**

← His green smoothie

Sure, that's tomato juice

← Always with the merch!

← Definitely stolen property

Captain Fluffykins' **booming** evil cat laugh is not just blasting from the screen. It's also coming from OUTSIDE!

I race to the rooftop helipad and look up to the night sky.

'THIS CAN'T BE HAPPENING!'

But it **IS!**

And if you thought **SATURDAY** was staggering, just wait until ...

FUN FACTS

WITH JUSTIN CHASE

ROCK, PAPER, SCISSORS is one of the oldest hand games ever, with the original version dating back to the Chinese Han Dynasty (206BC–200AD). Over time there have been variations around the world using different elements including **Elephant, Human, Ant** in Indonesia and **FROG, SLUG, SNAKE** in Japan.

I win. AGAIN!

The current hotdog eating **world record** is **76 HOT DOGS** in **TEN MINUTES**, set in 2021 by Joey Chestnut. Don't try this at home!

Gulp!

In the ancient **Olympics**, athletes competed **NAKED** as a tribute to the Greek God **ZEUS** and to show off their physique.

MOUNT RUSHMORE National Memorial is a massive sculpture of four former U.S.A. presidents carved into a granite mountain in South Dakota. It took **fourteen years** to create with 90% carved by DYNAMITE.

The first zombie movie, **WHITE ZOMBIE**, was released in 1932, not long after the first **Dracula** film.

Ancient Egyptians revered **CATS**. Wealthy families treasured them as pets, dressing them in **jewels**. When the cats died, they were MUMMIFIED and as a sign of mourning, the cat owners shaved off their own eyebrows.

The term **BOOBY TRAP** probably comes from the **seabirds** commonly known as **boobies**, named from the Spanish word 'bobo' meaning FOOL. They were **clumsy** and slow on ground, making them easy to catch. The birds were even known to land aboard ships, where they were readily caught then eaten by the crew.

HOW TO DRAW:
HAROLD CHASE

AKA Dad!

STEP 1
Start with two circles for eyes.

STEP 2
Add a dot in each circle for the pupil.

STEP 3
Curved lines for eyelids and a nose.

STEP 4
Draw the face around the eyes – a blobby shape joined to the nose by two curved lines

STEP 5
Now draw the hair and beard around the face. It can be a bit jagged in places.

STEP 6
Using four curved lines, draw a big smile – top lip, mouth, teeth and tongue.

STEP 7
Add two bushy eyebrows above the eyes using ragged lines.

STEP 8
Draw 'C' shapes for ears on each side of the face.

STEP 9
Add tiny strokes all over for hair texture and colour in the mouth.

WHAT'S <u>YOUR</u> PREDICTION FOR SUNDAY?

_____

_____

_____

_____

_____

_____

_____

Draw an illustration of Sunday.

AND NOW ... A BRIEF MESSAGE FROM

EVA & MATT

SHE WROTE
THE WORDS

UNI
EVA:
Nice hat!

HE WROTE THE
OTHER WORDS
AND DREW THE
PICTURES

UNI
MATT:
Twinning!

Hey there _____,

YOUR NAME HERE ◄ (Unless this is a library book. In that case,
just imagine your name here. Or use invisible ink).

You survived SATURDAY!* Congratulations. It was certainly
a jam-packed, epically sporty day, but we might just have
time to squeeze in one more game.

Wanna play Rock, Paper, Scissors? OK. Let's go. Pick one:

a) Paper

b) Scissors

c) Rock

d) All of the above**

Hey! You beat us. Well done!

* Well, we truly HOPE you survived
and didn't collapse in shock and are
currently rocking back and forth in the
corner upon seeing a Zombie Apocalypse
and/or Justin's dad spinning naked
during the Hammer throw.

** Oi! No cheating!

You may find this hard to believe, but neither of us are very sporty. We didn't win any sporting trophies growing up, although Eva did get medals for spelling and Matt did get ribbons for drawing. (We ended up studying Visual Communication at University, which is where we met and had to wear a silly hat when we graduated.)

In cross country races Eva would get lapped by the fast – AND slow – runners because she was just walking (and talking). And Matt always packed a book to read on sports day! Even though there were no first places, we still gave everything a shot and had fun. You don't have to be the winner to have a good time. (But winning is cool!)

Anyway, we hope you NEVER have a week like Justin's and if, on the off chance, there is a Zombie Apocalypse, that you make it to the higher ground.

Best wishes,

Eva ♡ Matt ☺

P.S. Always read the fine print!

P.P.S. Keep reading! Fine print AND books! The best way to try out lots of books is to be a member of your local library. Can you believe there are FREE books just waiting for you to borrow them? OK, so you do have to return them, but then you can borrow MORE free books! How amazing are libraries?! Answer: REALLY amazing!

P.P.P.S. Brace yourself for SUNDAY! Only one day left!!

EVA AMORES is a designer/photographer who has worked for the Sydney Opera House and the ABC. She was born in the Philippines and moved to Australia during high school. She likes shoes, travelling and more shoes.

MATT COSGROVE is the best-selling author/illustrator of *Macca the Alpaca* and the *Epic Fail Tales* series. He was born and raised in western Sydney. He likes chocolate, avoiding social interactions and more chocolate.

Eva and Matt met when they were randomly placed together for a group assignment at university twenty-five years ago and they've been collaborating ever since. They've made dinner, cakes, a mess, the bed, mistakes, memories, poor fashion decisions and two actual humans, but this is their first book series together.

When they were in lockdown and the world felt a bit grim, they could have mastered sourdough or binge watched Netflix but, no, they decided to create this series instead - **THE WORST WEEK EVER!** (Sorry about that.)

Here's a photo of Eva and Matt so if you ever see them in real life you know to run in the opposite direction.

AS ZOMBIES
(in case there's a zombie apocalypse)